To: Dexter + Waverly

with love,
Linda MacLeod

Passports for Pets

Linda Marie MacLeod

This is a work of informational fiction.

Copyright © 2017 Linda Marie MacLeod

All Rights Reserved. No part of this book may be reproduced in any form or by any means, electronically or mechanically, without prior written permission of the author.

Library of Congress-in-Publishing Data

MacLeod, Linda Marie
Passports for Pets
LCCN: 2017902353
ISBN – 13: 978-1542617499
ISBN – 10: 1542617499

Cover: Abstract Art by Bobbie McMonagle
Formatting by: Chad Millam
Illustrations by Andy Valenty
Author's email: lmariemac@yahoo.com

CreateSpace Independent Publishing Platform, North Charleston, SC
MacLeod, Linda Marie, Passports for Pets/Linda Marie MacLeod
Printed by Create Space, publisher for Amazon, U.S.A. Available on Amazon.com
Publication date 2017

For Professor Zengjun Peng

He met a Chinese dog once who was

having difficulty adjusting to life in America!

Meet the Pets!

1. MIMI - Beautiful and sophisticated - Paris, France to Los Angeles, California
2. MALCOLM AND MURDOCH - The troublemakers - Edinburgh, Scotland to Richmond, Virginia
3. BAOBAO - A shy diplomat - Beijing, China to Washington D.C.
4. BILLY - A big wave surfer - The Gold Coast, Australia to Honolulu, Hawaii
5. NOMSA - A fire fighter's best friend - Cape Town, South Africa to Alberta, Canada
6. VIKTOR - A mystery writer and actor - St. Petersburg, Russia to Minneapolis, Minnesota
7. CLEOPATRA - Of ancient heritage - Luxor, Egypt to Chicago, Illinois
8. BOLERO - A tango dancer - Buenos Aires, Argentina to Portland, Oregon
9. ROLF - A retired police dog - Stuttgart, Germany to Atlanta, Georgia

10. DIEGO - A university mascot and party animal -Puebla, Mexico to Austin, Texas

11. AASHKA - A yogi - Mumbai, India to Boulder, Colorado

12. HUE - Double meaning, 'Lily' and Imperial City - Phú, Vietnamto Orlando, Florida

13. THE CONVERGENCE NYC

MIMI

Chapter One

Andre and Nathalie Artois, French filmmakers, told their children Antoine and Sophie, ages six and eight, that the family was moving to Los Angeles, California. The children were sad to leave their friends, neighborhood, and cozy apartment. It wouldn't be easy to pack up toys, books, and clothes and move to a foreign country. Antoine and Sophie didn't know English.

   They were feeling anxious about making new friends and fitting-in at a new school. Questions about what life would be like, where they would live, and whether Californians would be friendly were on their minds.

They enjoyed Disney films like *Beauty and the Beast* and *The Lion King* so they reasoned moving to Hollywood might be fun. They were even promised a day at *Disneyland*.

Since Mimi, a beloved family member, was also immigrating to the U.S. the children felt a little better about moving. She was a French Poodle with masses of curly white fur coiffed or trimmed in the traditional style. Her collar sparkled with crystal jewels. On chilly days, she wore hand-knitted sweaters with blue and white stripes.

Mimi was sophisticated and stunningly beautiful with pedigree papers. That meant her parents were doggie royalty. She had a small black nose that pointed upward when she strutted down the famous *Avenue des Champs Elysées*.

Every day Mimi admired her reflection in the hall mirror before going out. The Artois' took her on long walks. They walked along the tree-lined Seine River and the many *belles promenades* or beautiful pathways throughout Paris.

Mimi was aware that something big was about to happen. But she was the last one to know what it was. Antoine and Sophie whispered among themselves and shed a few tears. All of their school friends and parents were invited for a party and it wasn't anyone's birthday. When the party was over everyone hugged and planted kisses on both cheeks, a French custom.

Mimi was wide-eyed and listened intently but she still didn't understand what was going on even though she was proficient in French; she barked the language and understood it perfectly. Everyone huddled together and whispered.

A few weeks later the mystery slowly unraveled. Mrs. Artois sorted through the family's belongings. Some were given to local charities and some were put into boxes. Mimi sat in her comfortable round velvet cushion all day just to make sure it wouldn't be given away. Whatever was happening, she had to have her cushion.

Then one day the unthinkable happened. A humongous truck pulled up. Four large men got out and rang the doorbell. They carried boxes and furniture out of the apartment and put them into the truck.

Suitcases were packed and soon a taxi pulled up to take the family to *l'Aéroport Charles de Gaulle*. Mimi looked around her familiar home one last time and tears trickled down her cheeks. She looked away so the children wouldn't see her. Mimi tried to be brave but she still wondered where they were going?

Mimi was too big to sit on Sophie's lap, so the airline crew put her in a large crate in the pet compartment. She fell asleep after take-off for the twelve hour flight across the Atlantic Ocean to the West Coast.

After they landed and picked up their luggage, the Artois family retrieved Mimi and took a limo to their new American home in suburban Los Angeles.

Mimi's first surprise was seeing a large fenced-in backyard with a swimming pool.

She chased after the happy squealing children. It was great to have a backyard of your own. In her opinion, however, French parks and gardens were far more beautiful. The Artois' seemed pleased with their new home.

Mimi stayed behind while the family went grocery shopping. She liked all-natural organic pet food and was worried about the quality of American food, the additives and preservatives.

The summer weather was too hot. The dogs she met walking on the sidewalks weren't friendly and none barked in French. They wouldn't play with her. They snickered when she passed by, growled, and then raced away.

When the family went to the ocean, Mimi cut her paws on broken glass scattered on the beach. She whined all night and wanted to return to Pairs. Antoine and Sophie missed their friends and their beloved France, too, so they weren't able to cheer her up.

Andre and Nathalie had to work immediately so they hired a French-speaking nanny for the summer. Miss Lucy was nineteen years old and a University of California Los Angeles (UCLA) student majoring in French and theatre. She was fun-loving. Antoine and Sophie liked her right away.

Mimi was happy because Lucy brought her energetic and playful Cocker Spaniel, Bud, along. He was easy going and cheerful. Mimi's sophistication and kind-of stuck-up demeanor melted the minute she saw Bud.

He wanted to play and they became fast-friends. Mimi liked Bud even though he didn't understand French. It didn't matter to her that they didn't speak the same language. Bud learned a little French from Lucy. He barked "*Bonjour*" meaning hello, trying to sound like Lucy's French tapes.

Lucy brought materials to build a miniature stage with a curtain for a puppet show. She played *The Music Man* on her iPod and taught the children to sing *Seventy-Six Trombones*. Antoine and Sophie marched the puppets on parade. Mimi and Bud were in the play, too. Mimi pulled the curtain open with her teeth.

And Bud welcomed the neighbor kids, Abbie, Ben, Clark, and Dani by doing doggie tricks.

After the show Lucy served a lunch of *pain au chocolat* which was a *croissant* with chocolate, *Brie* cheese, apples, and ice cold milk.

There were good times and bad in America which took a lot of getting used to. Mimi and the children didn't mind being immigrants after a while. Once you get to know people and they get to know you, the unfamiliar becomes familiar. Miss Lucy told the children to smile whenever they met other kids because smiling is a universal language. Mimi batted her eye lashes at Bud and barked, "*Nous allons jouer*" or "Let's play!" Bud jumped into the air and barked, "Chase me!"

MALCOM & MURDOCH

Chapter Two

Malcolm and Murdoch were two sassy little trouble-makers! They were West Highland Terriers known as *Westies* from Edinburgh, Scotland. The white fur on their heads stood straight up like an unruly cowlick on a kid. They had muscular chests like long distance swimmers and elongated bodies with short legs. The two M's were curious and bold, confident and affectionate.

    Malcolm and Murdoch took turns undoing each other's leashes. One pushed a stool to the back door and the other hopped up and unlocked it. Seconds later, they took off, rain or shine on a new adventure. They explored city parks and neighborhoods. Everyone knew them so they were always spotted quickly and recaptured.

Iona, their owner, admired their spunk and daring but sometimes they were too much to handle. She was the boss but they chose forgiveness rather than obedience.

Once they snuck onto a city bus and went to the *International Fringe Festival*. Actors wore theatrical makeup and bizarre costumes that thrilled them. Another time they ran around the neighborhood during a thunderous rain storm. The Westies' muddy fur was the same color as their dark brown eyes.

When Iona's friend, Gracie, came to visit, Malcolm and Murdoch zoomed through her legs out the front door. They heard an ice cream truck with carnival music. The neighborhood kids were running after it to buy treats. When the little ones dribbled, guess who was right there with their tongues hanging out? Malcolm and Murdoch never missed an opportunity!

Those two doggies were outrageous but Iona loved them dearly. They were her family. The stunt that actually bothered her the most happened at the *Royal Edinburgh Military Tattoo*.

The annual event took place on the *esplanade* or open field of *Edinburgh Castle*. Bagpipers from all over the world entertained the spectators. They wore colorful plaid kilts, gigantic furry head dresses, sashes, spats, and military medals.

The grounds dazzled with bright lights and fireworks! The crowd's energy, applause and cheers were contagious.

She told the boys, as she called them, that she was going to the event. Malcolm and Murdoch sulked for hours because they wanted to go too.

In the past, they saw the show on the *telly* or television, but never from the stands, or underneath them. Iona refused to take them because they wouldn't pass the security check, or so she thought.

Malcolm and Murdoch conspired to go to the Tattoo by themselves. They stole some *pounds* or money from Iona's dressing table, put it in a pouch and hung it from their collars. Then they scooted into a taxi when a patron jumped out. Most taxis went to the castle on this night.

Once they arrived, they would try to smuggle themselves under a big lady's tent coat. They hoped she wouldn't giggle from their fur tickling her legs. No luck! No lady with an expansive garment showed up. They had to stay out of sight or get caught and be thrown out!

Finally a man with a beverage cart for the *Colour Guard* walked close to their hiding place. This was the chance they had been waiting for. They squeezed into the opening underneath the cart. Ice was stored there and it was freezing. When the cart came to a stop the M's adventure really began . . .

In the meantime, Iona arrived and took her seat in the bleachers. A handsome gentleman sat down next to her. He was from the U.S. Since this was his first trip to Scotland, he asked her many questions. She was proud of her heritage and told him all about Edinburgh and the Tattoo.

After the dignitaries were introduced and after *Trooping the Colour* or presenting the national flags, the military Drum Major was all-set to lead the first unit. Pipe, drum, and bugle players stood ready to march.

Malcolm and Murdoch shivered. They couldn't see anything from the cart. So, they pushed the door open and ran as fast as they could, through the ranks and up to the front line behind the Major.

Their tartan plaid wescot vests helped them blend in. The musical drills began and everyone marched forward. It was the only way to go. The M's imagined seeing themselves later on United Kingdom (UK) television. Stars at last!

As they led the parade everyone laughed except Iona who was horrified. Those naughty boys! She wondered what to do. By now she knew the first name of the American who sat next to her. She asked Ian to accompany her to security.

When the M's saw her they knew they were in big trouble. Iona paid a hefty fine for their unsanctioned entrance into the Scottish parade. She thanked Ian, scooped the dogs into her arms, and left as quickly as possible. There was complete silence on the way home.

Months later the *Clan Mackay of Borve Castle* in Sutherland gathered for the annual *Highland Games*. Iona attended. She wanted to relax and have fun. When she arrived it was foggy and damp from days of raining. She ordered some hot English tea, took a sip, looked up, and was surprised to see Ian.

This was the second time they met by chance. Ian had always wanted to attend a Clan Mackay reunion. And what a surprise, they had the same last name.

He asked about the Westies and Iona said they were staying with neighbors for the weekend. After having so much fun together Iona and Ian decided to keep in touch via email and on their smart phones.

One year later, Ian invited Iona to come to America for the *Pacific Northwest Highland Games*. The games were held the same week as the *National Tartan Day* in New York City. The *Empire State Building* was lit at night with hearts and flowers. It was April and it was springtime.

This was Iona's first trip outside the UK. Ian greeted her at the airport in Scottish with a heavy American accent. He said, "*Diadhuit, conásété,*" Hello, how are you? She laughed but appreciated his effort to speak her language.

Iona asked Ian what his favorite Scottish foods were because she was a great chef. He tried *haggis* the Scottish National dish, but wouldn't try *black pudding*. *Tatties* or *potato scones* tasted good and he liked all sorts of sausages. Shortbread *biscuits* or butter cookies were his favorite dessert.

Iona and Ian's friendship turned romantic. After spending time together, they never wanted to be apart. But where would they live? Would she be willing to move to the U.S.? Could he find a job in Scotland? Would Malcolm and Murdoch suffer from culture shock?

Ian lived in Richmond, Virginia. He owned an Irish pub in the downtown area. Iona could be the chef. Moving to America made more sense. Her English was pretty good but he couldn't understand the Scottish *brogue*.

They got married in an Edinburgh chapel. Mackay Clansmen raised their swords in an arch for the couple to pass under. He wore the Clan plaid *kilt* and she wore the Clan *tartan* banner over her white lace wedding dress. A lone bagpiper led the bridal party down a country lane to the reception. It was sunny in Scotland and everyone was delighted to celebrate with them.

The boys had to behave or be banished. No spilled champagne, no paws in the wedding cake, no opening of gifts, no running under tables, no bumping into guests, no exploring the castle, no licking the bride and groom or running around them during their first dance!

Malcolm and Murdoch behaved surprising well at the wedding. They overheard Iona tell Ian that if the M's stayed out of trouble, they could go with them on their honeymoon to the Caribbean Island of St. Thomas.

The newlyweds had a suite and the M's had a room of their own. The M's kept busy as usual. They shimmied down the balcony at sunset to check out the gorgeous beach and to watch people getting off cruise ships. Malcolm and Murdoch enjoyed the attention from the passengers. They were adorable after all!

No matter what life would be like in a new country, they were ready. They didn't understand American English very well but never had any problem making their wishes known.

Their 'cuteness' pretty much got them anything they wanted. Iona would make sure they liked American doggie food. The house would be theirs during the day. So they had lots of time to plan new adventures.

At the doggie park they heard that first responders, like police and firemen, were just minutes away. That gave them the confidence to run wild! They were not one bit afraid of the unknown and they had each other!

One question remained, was America ready for them?

BAOBAO

Chapter Three

Baobao was a Chow Chow from Beijing, China. She had a body of abundant fur and a lion's mane that framed her large head. In Chinese *chow* means puffy lion dog. BaoBao's deep-set dark eyes were vigilant; she saw everything. Her straight back legs allowed her to waddle like a fashion model down a runway. She was built for endurance not speed and enjoyed long walks around the capital city.

A blue-black tongue was proof of her ancient royal heritage. She was fiercely independent and proud. BaoBao was fluent Mandarin. She could bark it and comprehend it. Noodles, steak, seaweed and fish were her favorite foods! After dinner one night she could tell something was up . . .

She discovered her family would be relocated to the U.S. with diplomatic privileges. Zhāng Lihua, a brilliant multilingual scholar and single mother was appointed the Chinese Ambassador to the U.S. Lihua told her 12 year-old daughter, Lin, they were moving to Washington D.C.

Shortly after their arrival *the President's Portuguese Water dogs, Bo and Sunny* invited BaoBao to a picnic lunch on the south lawn of the *White House*. Lihua and Lin dropped off BaoBao because they had appointments to see brownstones in Georgetown. A state dinner was planned for them later that night.

The only word Bo and Sunny knew in Mandarin was "*Nîhâo*," or hello. BaoBao was savvy. She could bark hello in many languages but only looked away. She didn't want any new friends no matter how high-up they were in the government.

BaoBao refused to run and play; she just sat in the shade with droopy lips and pouted until the Zhāng's returned.

Bo and Sunny were used to international guests. They were outgoing and friendly. Their chef prepared a special treat for BaoBao but she refused to try it.

Bo and Sunny ran freely through the White House without the *Secret Service*. They showed BaoBao their hiding places. They showed her the *Oval Office* and the *Lincoln* bedroom. BaoBao wasn't interested in American history. She shuffled behind them, felt like an outsider, and wanted to go home.

That night BaoBao wondered how long they would have to stay in the U.S. She had a bad dream. She was trapped in a house without any windows or doors. There were no noodle vendors, no fish markets, no familiar faces and nothing good to eat. In the morning, she found out that Lin brought a case of delicious Chinese dog food with her. But how long would it last?

When the Chinese food ran out BaoBao became more and more depressed. She sat around all day and sulked. She didn't want to do anything.

Sometimes, Lin would take her for walks after school. A slow stroll in *Montrose Park* always cheered her up. She watched grey squirrels climb up and down oak trees shaking acorns to the ground. Cardinals and blue jays flew overhead singing and chirping. She thought Chinese birds were prettier. And they sang hypnotic tunes that stuck in your head and gave you good dreams.

Lin became busy with homework and piano lessons. Days came and went without BaoBao's walk. She hoped they would return to China soon. It's what kept her going. Then one day she whimpered and whined for hours. She dragged her back legs and crawled forward using her front paws.

She would escape when the heavy wooden door opened. BaoBao clenched her Chinese passport in her teeth. Lin saw her and said, dear

BaoBao, Georgetown is our home now. We're not ever returning to China. THAT DID IT!

BaoBao stopped eating and the Zhāng's took her to a doggie counselor. Dr. Jung said BaoBao's case was challenging but not impossible. He would help BaoBao adjust to being an immigrant even though the culture, language, and food were strange to her. BaoBao was uncooperative and had no interest in becoming an American. But, Dr. Jung had an idea.

He found an excellent Chinese doggie chef who recreated BaoBao's favorite dishes. Chef Wu was famous for creating the best Asian doggie meals in the West. At first BaoBao wouldn't try the food. But it really smelled good. Once she tasted it, she gobbled it down.

Dr. Jung also enrolled BaoBao in an international support group for foreign dogs with diplomatic privileges. The dogs came from around the world. They barked in English, exchanged stories, watched foreign films, played in doggie parks, and were trained in English commands.

These dogs had a lot in common. Some were shy at first but over time they all felt at ease. BaoBao became a little happier when she got to know the other dogs. These friendships diminished her loneliness and isolation. The doggie friends shared their struggles and formed lifelong friendships. Their owners even arranged playdates on the weekends.

BaoBao cheered-up even more when Lin took her to see the famous giant panda by the same name at the *National Zoo*. Seeing the panda chewing bamboo leaves reminded her of China. She exhaled a long slow breath. If the *panda, BaoBao* could be happy, maybe she could be happy, too. Lin didn't tell her that the panda would be relocated to Chengdu to meet her new boyfriend.

BaoBao would give her new country a chance. She wondered however, if Bo and Sunny would give her another chance? Lihua sent a note for her. Maybe life in Washington D.C. wouldn't be so bad after all!

BILLY

Chapter Four

Billy from Australia was a true Aussie, to the core. He lived to surf on the Gold Coast. Most beagles have their noses on the ground and their tails in the air. These dogs have a natural tracking instinct. However, Billy could be seen with his nose in the air and his tail on the ground as he rode the BIG WAVES.

His best mate or friend, Bailey Brown, was an expert surfer and he lived to surf, too. Bailey made Velcro™ booties for Billy that stuck to Velcro™ patches on his small surf board. Bailey and Billy rode the waves when the surf was in. Billy was trained and certified as a surf-lifesaver. When surfers took a bad tumble, Billy fearlessly dove into the ocean to rescue them. He was small but he had powerful lungs because Bailey trained him hard to swim as a puppy. They were inseparable. They were like brothers.

The international surf community was like a family. And surfers from around the world got to know each other when they competed at *World Surf League* events like the *Big WaveAwards*, *Waves4Water*, or the *Billabong Ride of the Year* in Mainland Mexico.

Sometimes Bailey competed on the long board where swells rose between six and ten feet high. Some of his favorite competitions were *J-Bay* or *Jeffrey's Bay*, South Africa, *Cow Bombie*, Western Australia, and the *North Shore* of Oahu, Hawaii.

Riding the waves was thrilling and sometimes dangerous! Surfers had to be in top physical condition, excellent swimmers and knowledgeable in oceanography.

After surfing all day Billy and Bailey gathered with friends on the beach for a sunset barbecue. Dylan strummed his guitar and sang ballads about natural beauty. After a supper of grilled fish and vegetables, Billy and Bailey drove home with their surfboards tied to their brightly painted yellow jeep, their faces flushed from the sun and wind.

    The next morning, Bailey worked on his computer. He bought and sold surfboards on *E-Bay*. He was a master carpenter, crafted high quality boards, and sold them in his surf shop, 'Waves Forever.' Everyone on the Gold Coast knew Billy and Bailey and liked them.

    On one of their trips to Hawaii, Bailey visited a customer, Akamu Kalani. He and his father owned one of the largest surf shops on the Island. Akamu met with Bailey and his father to discuss a business partnership.

    Billy played hide and seek with some local kids in the front yard while the meeting that was going on would change their lives . . .

    After they returned home, Bailey seemed busier than usual. He hired a sales associate to work in his shop and an accountant to manage the cash and pay the bills.

Billy was enrolled in an advanced course for detecting scents. He learned how to smell ocean predators, like sharks. He already had a certification in life saving. Billy was always welcome in the worldwide surfing community.

He was surprised when Bailey packed up their stuff for yet another trip to Oahu. And Billy was unaware that his new skills would soon be tested. They rented a small beach home needed for a longer stay rather than just for a vacation or surfing event.

Hawaii was tropical and in some ways similar to Australia. People spoke English in both countries. The Aussie accent sounded different than American English. Billy didn't always understand the Hawaiian accent. Sometimes he would stare at islanders with a blank look until they repeated their words.

Luckily, the seafood was delicious and the tradition of beach barbecues continued. New friends were easily made because ocean- loving people stuck together.

However, Billy felt sad when the days stretched into weeks and the weeks into months. He wondered when they were going home. His heart ached and he was sick to his stomach. Billy was homesick and didn't know why. Everyone was nice. He had a comfortable bed, tasty food, and his best mate was nearby. He still wanted to cry.

Then one day something terrible happened! Billy and Bailey were surfing on the big waves. All of a sudden, Billy noticed that Bailey had disappeared. When he went down, he always resurfaced quickly. This time was different. After a few minutes, Billy SMELLED it.

A large killer shark had taken a big bite out of Bailey's board. Bailey swam for his life away from the shark as fast as he could. Billy smelled another shark in the aqua waters. He had to do something.

He took a deep breath, and rode a smaller wave in Bailey's direction. He got there just in time to rescue Bailey who climbed onto Billy's board. Together they rode the waves and then paddled into the shallow waters.

Both surfers were shaking and felt like throwing up but they were happy to be safe and alive. Billy was a hero! A reporter from the *Honolulu Star-Adviser* interviewed Bailey.

After this near-tragedy, Bailey became more and more homesick, too. He missed his friends and family in Australia. Even though Hawaii was called paradise and living there was fun, it still wasn't home to these two mates.

Bailey worked out a deal with his Hawaiian partners. They agreed to continue working remotely via internet communications.

Bailey and Billy were immigrants for only two years. They understood why it was hard for people to move to a new country. When their transpacific jet landed at the Gold Coast Airport, they deplaned and slowly breathed in the Australian air in the land known as *Down Under*. Outside the terminal Billy kissed the ground, in his Beagle way, and the taxi cab driver said with a hardy laugh, "Welcome, *'ome mates*!"

NOMSA

Chapter Five

Nomsa was the new resident puppy and companion of Cape Town's fire and rescue service, District West. At one month old, she could fit in a fire helmet. When Nomsa was born her coat was pure white but after a few weeks black spots appeared.

Nomsa belonged to Chief Fire Officer Mosola Bello. She slept in a patchwork quilt-lined basket in his office. All the firefighters wanted to play with her.

When a fire alarm went off, Nomsa jumped on the sleeping firefighters to make sure they woke up. She was much more than a 'watch' dog, she was considered family. Dalmatians are very intelligent and loyal pets.

When the firefighters sponsored an open house as part of the community outreach, Nomsa demonstrated what to do when someone's clothes caught on fire. The battalion chief called out the commands and she obeyed. The children repeated after the chief: "**Stop** where you are, **Drop** to the floor, **Roll** around." This procedure smothers flames and saves lives.

When the firefighters got bored, they chased her around the station and played games like hide-an'-seek. In quiet times, Nomsa wandered around, untangled the hoses, or stuck out her tongue for a taste of stew.

Seriously, she had to be well-trained because it was a matter of life or death; safety or injury. When an alarm rung the firefighters jumped into their gear, slid down the brass pole, and climbed into the fire trucks. She went with them and sat on the front seat.

On one occasion, a little boy about eight years old, jumped out of the window of a burning house. Luckily, a fireman standing below caught him. While the firefighters searched for other family members he was put on a stretcher near the truck where Nomsa sat.

When he saw Nomsa, he thought he was seeing things. Puppies are so cute, especially ones wearing a red fire helmet and a matching bandana. Nomsa pressed her face against the window to prove that she was real.

The little boy smiled. Nomsa distracted him for a while. After what seemed like hours, the boy was put into a rescue vehicle for the hospital. He cried loudly and pointed at Nomsa. The chief let her out to comfort him. She laid on the stretcher next to him and the little boy fell asleep from exhaustion.

Afterwards, Chief Bello drove to the hospital, picked Nomsa up, and the two of them returned to the fire station. She was really hungry because she was growing fast and needed at least five small meals a day.

Nomsa thought stews, *maize porridge*, and *biltong*, a dried meat like jerky made by the firemen were much better than ordinary dog food. On special occasions, they barbecued or *braaid* meat. Nomsa loved the smell and taste of grilled steak.

When the Cape Town firefighters were asked to help Canadian firefighters in Alberta they didn't hesitate. Wild fires blazed out of control for months and the local firefighters needed relief. Before they entered the burning forest, the South Africans sang and danced for good luck. Nomsa, now fully grown, went with them to cheer-up the Canadians.

Nomsa was striking with her black spots popping out against her pure white coat. She wore a light-weight red helmet with a chin strap to keep it in place. Everyone was happy to see her!

Canada is a long way from South Africa. And Nomsa couldn't wait to smell the ocean, to smell the grilled and stewed meats, and to smell the clean smoke-free air . . .

As the firefighters prepared to leave Canada, the Chief broke some bad news to Nomsa. His voice sounded weak and his eyes were misty. The Canadians asked if Nomsa could stay in

Canada. They had never seen such a well-trained dog. A large donation was offered to the Cape Town Firefighters' favorite charity for orphans.

The chief didn't want to leave Nomsa behind. But the Canadians lost so many lives fighting fires that he believed it would serve the greater good if Nomsa stayed.

Back in the Cape Town fire station, her empty bed pained the chief. It had to be removed. Nothing could make up for her absence.

As for Nomsa, she figured out very soon what was going on. For now, she worked in Canada but she would probably get sent to the U.S. Wherever firefighters battled flames, she would serve.

In fact, wild fires were ripping through Washington state and California. Thousands of homes and forests were being destroyed. A lengthy drought made the situation even worse.

Nomsa focused on the firefighters' morale and tried to keep their spirits up. She never dwelled on the past but she never forgot where she came from.

Someday the South Africans would be asked for help again. When that day came, she would welcome them with all her heart! Nomsa means 'faith' in the *Xhosa* or *Bantu* language of South Africa. She would keep that faith.

Note: Class of 2013 Cape Town Fire & Rescue by Tertius Nagel, 1-3-14 YouTube, South African Wildland Firefighter Tribute Waving Flag by Jeandre Van Heerden,7-26-14, YouTube,ToughestFirefighterAliveCompetition: The Hose Run, Obstacle Course, Tower, Stair Climb

VICTOR

Chapter Six

Irina Romanov was a Russian ballerina who loved Nicolai Tolstoy, a world-class concert pianist. Irina's company performed at *Northrop Auditorium at the University of Minnesota*. At the same time Nicolai was invited to play as a guest artist with the *Minnesota Symphony, at Orchestra Hall*, Minneapolis.

They studied English as children and wanted to visit the U.S. for many years. Nicolai was an orphan and Irina was his best friend. Someday, he hoped to marry her. Romanov and Tolstoy talked about living in the U.S. if they could immigrate legally.

After their Minneapolis performances, they flew to the *U.S. Consulate in Chicago* and applied for entry. It was granted because they had no problem earning a living and contributing to American society. They celebrated by enjoying a candlelit dinner at a fine restaurant.

Afterwards, Irina became quiet and looked sad. Nicolai asked her what was wrong. She said she was worried about her Russian Spaniel, Viktor. It wouldn't be easy to bring him to America because he didn't have visa privileges.

Viktor was staying with Irina's sister, Natasha and her husband Yakov in St. Petersburg on the Neva River. The Neva flows into the Gulf of Finland and to the Baltic Sea. Cruise ships dock at the Sea Station, *Morskov Vokzul.*

Nicolai used a secure server to send an internet message to Natasha with a plan for Viktor's extraction.

An intelligence operative or a spy, dressed like an American tourist in a bright blue jogging suit, met Natasha, Yakov, and Viktor on a side street near the *Gamma Coffee (кофе) shop.*

It was midnight and Viktor had no clue what was going on. Natasha packed his favorite toys and blanket in a small portable kennel. They petted him and said, "*ПОКа*" which means "Bye Bye" in Russian!

Viktor and the spy boarded a cruise ship for Southampton, England. An officer from the British Secret Service met the ship. He escorted Viktor to Heathrow Airport for a flight to Minneapolis/St. Paul.

Irina and Nicolai met Viktor at the baggage carousel with balloons, flowers, and doggie treats. The thimble-full of vodka he had been given for the trip had completely worn off. He blinked his eyes, yawned several times and barked, "*Privyet*" or "Hello."

He had jetlag but was so happy to see Irina that he jumped into her arms and nuzzled her in the chest. Viktor noticed that everyone in the terminal spoke a strange foreign language. Irina said it was English.

Their new home was now in the middle of America. She petted and kissed him on the forehead and then wrapped him in a soft blanket and carried him to the car.

Irina and Nicolai purchased a townhome near the Mississippi River in the Minneapolis warehouse district. Nicolai taught piano at *MacPhail Center for Music* and performed with symphonies throughout the U.S. Irina danced professionally with the Minneapolis-based *Zenon Dance Company.*

As for Viktor, he missed Russia but he decided that wherever Irina lived, he wanted to live. The next morning, Irina and Nicolai had big news for Viktor. They were getting married and he was in the wedding party. He would wear a tailor-made tuxedo vest and sashay down the aisle with their wedding rings on a satin pillow.

After the wedding, a doggie sitter would take him back to the townhome for a scrumptious dinner and a movie. Viktor loved American doggie movies like, *Benji, The Shaggy Dog,* and *Turner & Hooch.* And since Viktor was a budding actor in Russia, maybe he could land a part in a film or on the stage. The whole family was *artsy.*

When he woke up the next morning he was alone with the sitter; no Irina, no Nicolai. They went on a honeymoon without him. It was clear he had to share Irina with her new husband. He didn't like it but Nicolai was a good guy and Irina was happy.

He made friends with his dog-walker, Lara, another Russian immigrant. She translated his memoir into English so other immigrant dogs could learn about his adventure in Minnesota.

Viktor adjusted slowly to his new home in the U.S. Some immigrants move here for a better life or for jobs. He wasn't sure if life would be better. On the other hand, he wasn't worried about being a *starving artist* because Irina would feed him.

Even so, Viktor wanted to contribute to the family. He worried that it would be difficult to get published or to land a part in a film or play! Still, he was talented, worked hard and learned fast.

While he waited to audition for a part in *Peter Pan* at the *Children's Theatre,* he wondered what happened to the man with the royal blue jogging suit. The spy wore sunglasses, never said a word and then disappeared! Viktor would write a novel about him!

CLEOPATRA

Chapter Seven

Cleopatra, Cleo for short, was a *Pharaoh Hound* from Egypt. The Pharaoh hound has been around since 4,000 – 3,000 BC. This breed was known for hunting, guarding, and working in the military as a soldier's companion. The ancient Egyptian word for dog is *iwiw* which means bark.

   Cleo was a sight-hound and a scent- hound. She was a long-distance runner. She ran very fast and jumped very high. Cleo was tall, slender, and athletic. Her neck was long and lean and her head was wedge-shaped and chiseled. She had small oval eyes, large ears, and a whip-like tail with a white tip.

Cleo had a pleasant disposition and was devoted to her owners, Babu Minyawi and Bahiti Suyuti. The three of them were best buddies. She loved Babu and Bahiti but was shy of strangers. They made her feel uncomfortable. Cleo was healthy and happy living in Luxor. Given her ancient heritage it was no wonder that she liked Luxor's temples, ruins, and tombs. Luxor is near the ancient city of Thebes, close to the Nile River and the *Valley of the Kings*. The *University of Chicago's Oriental Institute* is also located in Luxor.

Babu was an archeologist and an expert on Egyptian antiquities. His wife, Bahiti, had many interests including photography, painting, and studying architecture. They were in their 60's with no children. Babu worked at the *Chicago House in Luxor*.

Unexpectedly, he received an offer to teach at the *University of Chicago*, during the 90th *archeological field season*. The Dean thought his field experience would provide a valuable contribution.

Bahiti secured a position as a curator of ancient artifacts at the *Chicago Institute of Art*. Cleo was considered an important member of the family. Would she adjust to leaving her homeland and beloved culture? She was a homebody and her roots were deeply planted in Egypt.

The couple bought a home nestled between the university campus and *Jackson Park*. Their Egyptian and Middle Eastern art work and furnishings helped them feel at home. The backyard had a high fence to keep Cleo from jumping over it.

A student from the university tract team exercised Cleo. Running fast and far was part of her daily routine.

Babu and Bahiti didn't understand why Cleo wasn't distressed about the whole moving ordeal. She seemed preoccupied. Cleo had something else on her mind . . .

As the weeks passed and the seasons changed from summer to autumn, it was obvious that Cleo was changing, too! Her energy-level slowed down and her tummy seemed to expand. Soon it became obvious that Cleo was expecting puppies. It surprised everyone!

On Thanksgiving Day the family welcomed five new puppies. The three female puppies were named, Alexandria, Siwa, and Sinai and the two male puppies were called Aswan and Ra. Cleo barked *"Ha-i"* and *"Ahlan"* in *Arabic* which is an Egyptian greeting.

She was very busy feeding and caring for her babies. At first Cleo wasn't thinking about the geographic or cultural differences between America and Egypt. Then she realized these new pups were U.S. not Egyptian citizens. That worried her. Could she communicate with them in Arabic as they grew? She understood informal Arabic and very little English. All the doggies at the park only barked in English.

The puppies were athletic and good-natured like their mother. They grew quickly during the first few months. Then, one evening after Batu and Bahati came home from work they made an unexpected announcement.They told Cleo that some of the puppies would have to be given away.

No matter how sweet they were or how long they petted her, she wouldn't hear of it. Cleo shed big puppy-dog tears and barked that she wouldn't give any of them up. However, there just wasn't room for five puppies and Cleo in the same home.

Cleo wanted to run away and take the puppies with her. She knew she couldn't and anyway Egypt was oceans away. It seemed hopeless.But in her heart she knew that there was always hope.

Batu and Bahati had many Egyptian friends at the university, the Art Institute, and the Chicago House. Bahati recorded adorable videos of Cleo and the puppies while they played and relaxed in their doggie beds. He posted them on social media.

Bahati wanted to find good Egyptian homes for the puppies. Egyptians would appreciate Cleo's heritage and they could teach the puppies Arabic. The story and video created a lot of interest and went viral.

Soon offers to take the pups surfaced via email. Bahati and Cleo interviewed the prospective new owners. Once they saw the handsome puppies they all wanted them. Two families took two puppies each. The siblings would grow up together. The fifth puppy, Alexandria, stayed with her mother.

It was hard to say goodbye, but everyone promised to stay in touch. Cleo's family met at Jackson Park for long walks on Saturdays. There were competitions in the 50 yard dash and Siwa and Sinai helped train their owners for the *Chicago Marathon*.

This new generation of runners was superfast just like their Mom and ancient relatives. Cleo was proud of her offspring and happy to build a new life with her family!

BOLERO

Chapter Eight

La Cumparsita (1916) was one of Bolero's favorite songs with its syncopated rhythm and romantic melody. Besides an 'old world' *bandoneón*, similar to an accordion, a tango *orquesta tipica* could have a violin, piano, bass, flute or guitar. In Spanish, *Bolero* means dancing.

Since the internationally popular tango began on the streets of Argentina, it's only fitting that Bolero, who was rescued from the streets of Buenos Aires, would be called *El baile del perrito* or dancing doggie.

Sofia Perez and Romero Santiago, her tango partner, found Bolero on el *Caminito*, a street in the *Boca District*. He glanced up at them with melancholy eyes that seemed to say, please take me home with you. They always wanted a dog but their schedule at the dance studio kept them far too busy to care for a pet.

Bolero was a medium-built Golden Retriever with medium length hair and a calm disposition. In the early morning hours when they found him, his coat was caked with the mud and dust of a big city. Bolero was hungry and weak. He ate scraps from garbage cans and drank rainwater from gutters.

He didn't bark *Hola* or hello. He only whined in a whisper. Bolero followed the couple for several blocks keeping a safe distance, camouflaged by the shadows.

When the dancers reached their garden-level apartment, Bolero looked up at them again with longing. Sofia spoke quietly to Romero. He petted Bolero gently while Sofia opened the door and switched on an outdoor lantern.
It was unanimous! Bolero was welcome for the night. A blanket was placed on the floor for him and soon after, all three fell fast asleep.

When the late morning sun forced its way through the wooden blinds, Bolero barked loudly waking up Sofia and Romero. They were startled because they forgot about him. Once fully awake they remembered bringing the Retriever home in the twilight hours.

Sofia smelled something nasty and as soon as Bolero was fed he was scrubbed in a washtub on the patio and rinsed with a garden hose. After the bath, he basked in the warm sunshine and chewed on a bone.

Since Bolero didn't have any identification they went to a city shelter to make sure no one reported a missing pet. It turned out he was homeless.

Sofia and Romero decided to adopt him. They treated him like family and named him, Bolero because his whine reminded them of a mournful violin and his slow stagger as he followed them home was like a sleepy-eyed tango dancer. His name was perfect and became a premonition of what was to come . . .

Sofia and Romero owned a small dance studio. They taught 3rd and 4th graders tango on Saturdays. Many tourists also found their way to the studio for lessons. On Friday and Saturday nights the dance instructors performed at area night clubs and at *milongas*.

Sofia danced in strappy high heels and mid-calf length fancy dresses with a side-slit for movement and kicks. The pair danced together since childhood. It was easy for them to move as one counter-clockwise on the hardwood dance floor under dimmed chandeliers.

Bolero was needy. He wanted attention and didn't want to stay home alone. They brought him to the studio and trained him to sit quietly in the back of the room. He was a very intelligent dog who was fond of people, especially children who loved him right back.

Sofia noticed that Bolero tapped his front paws to the rhythmic music as he sat there. After the last lesson, Sofia played some tango music and invited Bolero to dance. At first she taught him to follow in slow syncopated four-

four time. They danced completely relaxed in the empty studio. Bolero swayed with the music. He was a natural. Sofia moved her feet and hips in a backward *ocho*. That's a curvy movement like skating backwards. Bolero gently pushed forward to maintain the connection. They had a lot of fun!

Romero entered the room and when he saw them together it gave him an idea. He had seen lots of dogs from Argentina dancing tango routines on *YouTube*.

Romero and Sofia trained Bolero in the art of tango dancing. He thrived and was happy and healthy. He enjoyed dancing as much as spending time with his new best friends. Even more surprising, he became an essential addition to the children's lessons. His rhythm was perfect. He tapped-out the timing for the children with his paws. Bolero demonstrated the 'tango walk' across the floor as the children giggled.

Bolero liked to be petted on his head, his back, or his belly after lessons. He was very professional and never, ever, licked anyone's face even if he liked them a lot. Licks and kisses were reserved for Sofia and Romero. Life was brilliant!

Then one day Romero announced he wanted to make a video of Bolero dancing. Sofia hired a seamstress to fashion a tango tux for Bolero in his favorite color, metallic blue, with a matching crystal collar. He sparkled! And the video was seen worldwide on the internet.

No one could have guessed what happened next! Bolero was an overnight sensation. Offers came in from around the world for Sofia and Romero to teach tango. The public believed this tango-team could teach anyone to dance, even people with two left feet.

Sofia and Romero weren't interested in relocating but an offer came from Portland, Oregon that they couldn't refuse. They decided to move to the U.S.

Bolero had grown accustomed to the 'good life' in Argentina. Every day he took a long *siesta* or nap, after a lunch of spicy street food like grilled *chorizo* on bread with *chimichurri* sauce.

He danced to Argentine music and trained with the students. At night he joined a group of doggie friends and their walkers. He stayed at home during Sofia and Romero's late night performances. But no matter how late, he greeted them warmly when they came home.

When Romero took Bolero's picture and presented it to the Argentine Embassy along with a doggie passport application, Bolero knew something was about to happen - but he never guessed they were moving to a new country!

ROLF – "DeutscherScherhund"

Chapter Nine

The Dieter boys found out their family was moving to the U.S. on Christmas day. The fifteen year old twins Kurt and Karl were mad about it; not crazy, happy, excited, but angry and glum. Lucas, 12, and Leon 10, didn't know what to expect and didn't want to leave Stuttgart, either.

    Mr. Dieter was the sales manager for *Porsche-Volkswagen* and Mrs. Dieter was the design-engineer for new models. They were being relocated to the *USA Headquarters* in Atlanta, Georgia.

    All four boys excelled at European football known as soccer in the U.S. Their league was undefeated and the boys won lots of trophies over the years. Kurt and Karl were sports heroes to their younger brothers. In fact, the whole family took soccer seriously.

The twins knew everything would be different in a new country. It wouldn't be easy switching schools as teenagers. What if there was no soccer in their new high school? Would American kids like them or make fun of their German accent? The Dieter children took English in primary school but had trouble with pronunciation.

What would Atlanta be like? Perhaps an internet search would provide some answers. The boys were so worried about themselves that they completely forgot about Rolf.

Rolf was a retired German Shepherd police dog. He stood 2 ½ feet tall and weighed nearly 80 pounds. Rolf's ears were always pointed straight-up like antennas. He smelled danger even if it was blocks away. His coat was thick and coarse; black, white, and silver.

Rolf was a detective; a criminal apprehender and a crime-solver. He was tenacious – that meant he never gave up while tracking a bad guy. He was loyal to his superiors. Even in retirement, he was always on-duty and slept with one eye open.

Rolf understood commands in German, not English. Most dogs know about 100 words, but Rolf's vocabulary stretched to 300. He was a genius! He preferred to eat German *wurst* or sausage and was known to down a *bier* (beer) on special occasions. Rolf's bark was deep and loud.

The whole neighborhood woke up if he barked a warning. Rolf was perceptive. He had a sixth sense but he didn't have a clue that the Dieters were moving.

The family arrived in Atlanta when the summer temperatures reached double-digits. The boys enrolled in *Concordia Language Camp* in northern Minnesota. They wanted to improve their English and cool off swimming in a glacier-formed lake.

Rolf was alone and confused. He wasn't sure why his family moved to the U.S. and he was not consulted about it either. There were no friendly or unfriendly faces in the neighborhood; he saw no one at all. No Dieter boys, no police officers, no criminals.

Rolf was fearless but without a mission he was bored. What would he do in America? Would he become an old house dog? He enjoyed *Sherlock Holmes'* episodes on public television (*PBS*) even though he didn't understand English. He figured out the story from the action. Rolf thought Sherlock would have solved more crimes with his help.

In Germany, he received numerous medals for bravery. But now, Rolf wanted to cry buckets although his pride and tough demeanor wouldn't let him. Living in Atlanta made him feel lost. He never went for walks. Instead, he crouched on the cool ceramic tile floor near the front door; his head rested on his front paws. This was how he spent the long hot days.

All of a sudden he heard something. His ears perked up. He held his breath and slowly crept closer to peek through the door's sidelight. Maybe it was a burglar or an armed intruder. He would save the day!

Just as a stranger in shorts began to slide letters into slot next to the door, Rolf barked loud and fierce! His growl could scare a dozen criminals away. False alarm! It was only the mailman who fell down the steps backwards in fear from Rolf's unexpected bark and the sight of his incisor fangs pressed against the narrow window. The mailman's heart pounded fast but he was not injured. There was a letter in the mailbox for Rolf.

It was from the Stuttgard police chief, Herr Schmidt. Rolf was needed back in Germany for a mission. An international crime ring was stealing jewels worth millions of *euros* or European dollars. The thieves were stealing diamonds from fine jewelry stores in Paris, Munich, and Amsterdam. Instead of each country trying to capture them, a new task force from the

European Union (EU) called *Interpol* was organized.

Since Rolf was experienced with the best criminal conviction record in the canine unit, he was offered a large sum to catch the crooks. The Dieter's put Rolf on the next plane to Germany. He slept soundly knowing he would need a lot of energy to solve the case. The international law enforcement team retrieved him at the Frankfurt Airport. He was briefed and immediately put to work.

Rolf had a plan. He would track the suspects when they entered a store by their scent supplied by evidence from Interpol. He would patrol the sidewalks and doors. When the store owners sounded the security alarm, Rolf would chase, corner and catch the thieves. He would contain and guard them until the police arrived.

Rolf was a professional. He could tell if the thieves were armed and he knew exactly what to do in every situation. Rolf's picture was withheld from the newspapers to protect his identity. He fought crime all summer.

He felt useful and important. The chief of police gave him a medal for bravery and said, "*Braver Hund!*" (good dog). Rolf was also given a monetary reward which he donated to *Georgia Soccer* in Atlanta.

In September he returned to the U.S. when the days were cooler and the boys were in school. They would be the ones who needed him now. He loved them and was eager to accept that mission!

Señor Don Diego

Chapter Ten

Talk about personality – Señor don Diego was a high-spirited friendly Chihuahua who always insisted on being the center of attention. At weddings he led the mambo and danced on stage. He shook the *maracas* with his agile front paws keeping time with the *Mariachi* singers. At birthday parties he jumped high to head-butt the *piñata* but always let the children knock it down. He didn't like candy but he liked to see the them run for it.

Diego had short silky golden hair with white poofs on his forehead and paws. His head was shaped like an apple and his ears were large compared to the rest of him. A bicycle basket was just the right size for him.

Diego barked, *"Hola"* or *"Adios"* with a yippy high pitch. He never shut up. Diego's favorite foods were fish tacos and chicken enchiladas with a bit of spice. Diego lived in Puebla, a Spanish colonial city not far from *El Cuidad de Mexico*, the capital.

   The Garcia's, José Luis and Isabel, treated Diego like a son and they spoiled him along with their two-year old daughter, Anna. She chased Diego around the apartment and called him, "*Diego Perrito Amigo*" or little doggie friend.

   The Garcia's had a surprise for Anna and Diego. They cooked the family's favorite burritos and dished-up fried ice cream for dessert. After dinner they told Anna and Diego the news . . .

   José Luis and Isabel had been accepted at the *University of Texas, Austin*. They would study at the *Moody College of Communication*, *School of Journalism*. José Luis wanted to be a radio sports announcer and Isabel wanted to be a journalist. Isabel's mother lived in Austin and offered to babysit Anna and Diego.

   Diego frowned when he heard about that because he preferred to explore the campus. He was a city dog and worldly! Once the news set-in, Diego became so excited that he ran in circles chasing his short white tail. A new adventure in Texas; he thought it would be fantastic!

Austin was famously called 'weird' because of the artists, musicians, hippies and techies congregating on *South Congress*. It was also known as the music capital of the U.S. Diego imagined Texans in cowboy hats and boots, long-haired musicians, and brilliant high tech students. He bought a new doggie collar with Western motifs or designs and was looking forward to college life.

After they moved, Diego begged every day to go to UT with Isabel or José Luis. He wanted to check out the *chicas* or girls and the campus. Finally, they plopped him into a backpack and took him to a popular dog-friendly coffee shop. There were tables and chairs outside and the location was center campus.

It wasn't long before students noticed Diego. They petted and fawned over him. He loved it. A student called him, Señor Don Diego, Super

Hero! Diego became very popular on campus. And that gave him an idea. . .

The mascot for the UT football team was a *Longhorn* steer. When the team won a game the UT tower lit up in pumpkin, the school color. Diego petitioned to become a co-mascot with the Longhorn. Because of his growing popularity the request was granted.

He flew into the stadium in a drone and landed on the back of the Longhorn. Diego impressed fans as the *'Bat Hombre'* also known as *'Batman.'* The university band played the rouser or fight song just as the drone landed. Diego's black silk cape, bat wings, mask and head-gear made him appear fearsome and authentic. Even though he was small, he commanded attention. The crowd went wild!

Everyone clapped, screamed, and laughed; the football team, cheerleaders, band members, fans and even the administration. He reveled in the spotlight and was adored by the assembly.

Being the new guy on campus didn't bother him one bit. He was popular! Even *CNN* was there to capture Diego's début or first time appearance on the field. Isabel wrote an article for both the *Daily Texan* and the *Texas Travesty*, a humorous publication. José Luis interviewed Diego on *KVRX*, FM radio, first in Spanish and then with an English doggie translator.

Diego wondered how to cheer up Anna and Grandma Rosita. They stayed at home a lot and watched *Telemundo Español* or Spanish television. He had another great idea! He wanted to invite the football team and cheerleaders over for a fiesta! Diego's family said, "*Si*" to hosting the party and Grandma agreed to cook authentic (real) Mexican dishes.

At the party, everyone danced *Salsa*, a Latin style partner dance. And the cheerleaders fought over who could carry Diego on their shoulders. He barked, "Ladies please take your turn." He was in doggie heaven!

AASHKA

Chapter Eleven

Aashka and Master Singh practiced yoga. Singh was a yoga *guru* or teacher in an *ashram* or retreat just outside of Mumbai, India. People from all over the world came to this wellness center. They learnt about the spiritual and health benefits of yoga. Yoga unites the mind, body, and spirit. It's based on the *Hindu* religion.

    Sometimes during *Dhyana* or meditation, Aashka hummed a soft-sounding "*OM*" with the group. The students fixed their eyes on her striking face for balance during a *Tree Pose*. Every morning as the sun rose, Aashka tilted her head to the heavens in a *Sun Salutation*.

She sat quietly a few feet from Shiv at outdoor sessions under *Indian banyan* trees. Water circulated in a stone fountain with a lion head. It emptied into a basin and then flowed up and out again. The continuous whoosh calmed the spirit like a lake splashing under a dock. Peacocks wandered around. *Jasmine* flowers, *Sitar* music and *Sanskrit* chants created peace and harmony.

What made Aashka unique, like no other? She was a Pug; a very cute dog with a very ugly face that looked wrinkled with an upside-down smile. Pugs have big button-like eyes, stout noses, chubby undersized bodies and curled tails.

Aashka adored being petted and her coat was silky smooth to the touch. Aashka was Shiv's valued companion and *muse* or inspiration. On Saturdays, children, six to twelve, came for yoga lessons. Aashka greeted them at the front gate.

A sign hung around her thick neck with *Namaste* printed on it. The word comes from the Sanskrit meaning, welcome or '*I bow to you.*' As a sign of respect, Shiv placed his hands together over his heart, slightly bowed, and said, "Namaste" at the end of each class. All who attended yoga sought *Satya*or or *Truth*.

Aashka had no idea that Shiv received a letter from the U.S. that would change their lives forever.

The owners of a yoga wellness center in Boulder, Colorado invited Shiv to teach a series of workshops for teachers from across the country, all expenses paid. They would stay with a famous Chinese healer, Master Yu, who lived in the Rocky Mountains near Estes Park.

Now, Aashka would have two masters. Shiv would instruct yoga teachers at the Boulder center and facilitate their enlightenment and physical training.

Shiv and Aashka arrived in Colorado at the end of May. The crisp mountain air and clear sunny skies were a welcome relief from the heat and crowds of Mumbai. Shiv told Aashka that Americans need healing; they are stressed-out!

Aashka and Shiv were like missionaries. They brought the gift of knowledge and peace to others.

In India most people speak both Hindi and English because of *British colonial rule*. Aashka didn't need to learn a new language. New food wasn't an issue either because she wasn't fussy. Children and adults usually warmed-up to her. Still, she had many questions.

Would American yogis respect her? She heard they were yoga know-it-alls! Could dogs legally practice yoga in Colorado? Aashka was worried about being excluded from the sessions. Without yoga, life in the Rockies would be dull. She would be lost and feel useless.

Her fears came true when Shiv broke the bad news! Even though Boulder was dog-friendly, no dogs were allowed in the training sessions. Aashka would have to stay in the mountain-retreat without Shiv all day, every day.
How long would they have to live here she wondered? But, thinking positive was an important discipline for a yogi. She reasoned

that embracing this situation would be hard, not impossible.

Aashka thought about the positives: The rustic mountain home was comfortable, the food and water were plentiful, the pine trees and wildflowers were beautiful and Master Yu seemed nice.

After work Shiv spent quality time with Aashka. When he returned, she never left his side. They meditated daily before dusk in the wooded backyard listening to a gentle mountain stream. Life in America was peaceful. Life was good. Life was however, a little lonely. In her wisdom, Aashka knew that life was not perfect. It was what you made of it.

About the time she adjusted to life in Colorado, Shiv announced they would travel to other states to teach yoga. New Mexico was next. She thought they would return to India after a month in Colorado. The challenges of living in a foreign country continued. Aashka was barkless; in Hindi and in English!

After he taught in many different states, Shiv decided to stay in the U.S. But after he saw tears in Aashka's eyes, he changed his mind. Instead, the duo conducted workshops around the world and returned to Mumbai in the cooler months. A compromise was reached.

Workshops abroad were balanced with reunions at home which refreshed and renewed their energy. After all, yoga was about balance and harmony. And, Aashka taught Shiv that life was also about honoring relationships between loved -ones!

HUE - Fu Dog

Phu Quoc dogs – Xin Chào "Hello" from Vietnam!

Chapter Twelve

The name hue has two meanings. The Imperial City, Hue, is on the Perfume River. It's also called, Sông Huong. In 1993 the city was designated as a *UNESCO World Cultural Heritage* site. Hue is also a Vietnamese name meaning, Lily. *Phu Quoc* is a common dog breed found in Vietnam and in this story, Hue is her name.

   She belonged to a little boy named Dat Nguyen. Dat means accomplished in Vietnamese and Nguyen is pronounced, win. Dat, a child of mixed heritage, was born in Vietnam in 1969. His Vietnamese mother died giving birth to him and he never knew his father, an American soldier.

His grandfather and grandmother raised him and loved him with all their hearts. They stood up for Dat, gave him a good home, and always encouraged him to work hard and have a positive attitude. They lived in a small home in District One of Phú Lôc, a city on the South China Sea.

Dat loved going to school and he was an excellent student. The other kids called him bui doi (dirt or dust of the earth) and were cruel to him because he was an orphan of mixed heritage. Grandpa Hai encouraged him to forget about it and instead focus on learning.

And, then there was Hue. Hue offered companionship and unconditional love without wanting anything in return. She slept near Dat's cot every night. She greeted him eagerly with happy barks when he came home from school.

Grandma Hāo made his favorite dish, sour shrimp, on Dat's birthdays. The family practiced *Buddhism* and lived life based on *Buddha's* teachings. There was a small shrine to Buddha in the home where fruits and flowers were placed to honor their spiritual leader.

Dat grew up in Vietnam and when his faithful companion Hue grew old and died, he named every dog after her, Hue. So he always had a Hue in his life. Dat was happy and Hue was devoted to him just like all the Hue's that came before her.

When Dat grew up he worked in tourism and managed a fancy resort on the ocean in Phú Lôc. Guests came from all over the world because of the ground's tropical beauty and pristine beach! Yet, whenever Americans stayed at the resort, his heart ached. There was a void or emptiness in him that was calling him to his father's homeland.

The *Amerasian Homecoming Act of 1987* passed by the *U.S. Congress* allowed Dat to immigrate if he wanted to. The American part of him was a mystery. Vietnam was the only home that he and Hue had ever known. He had a lot to think about and would take his time.

He knew that only two percent of Amerasian children ever met their fathers. Still, America, "The land of the free and the home of the brave" entered his dreams over the years.

He finally bought a ticket to fly to the U.S. Hue travelled with him because Dat lacked the courage to go alone and he wouldn't leave her behind. She was an important part of his history, too.

Dat was 46 years old and it was time he checked-out the West. He was open-minded about what he might or might not discover. Dat was a little bit scared and excited at the same time.

Since many immigrants enter the U.S. through Ellis Island, New York, Dat decided his first stop would be there. He would see plays on *Broadway* and walk through *Central Park* with Hue. Next, they took a train to Washington D. C. to visit the *National Mall* and the *Vietnam Memorial*. After that they went to *Disney World* in Florida.

The theme park made him feel happy and carefree. He and Hue acted like kids and no one cared. *Epcot*, his favorite park, showcased world-wide countries, cultures, customs, and cuisines.

Florida's climate was similar to Vietnam's and near the ocean, too. The shrimp was fresh and plentiful.

Dat was surprised when he met Americans who emigrated here from all over the world. Every country and culture seemed to be represented. And he fit in as a man of two cultures and two countries.

There was a large network of friendly Amerasians in the Florida area. They gathered for picnics and *Vietnamese Dragon Festivals*. Dat bonded with them. For the first time in his life he felt like a whole person accepted by others. He decided that he would take America up on its offer to come home!

Hue surprised Dat when she barked in English after only a few weeks. She was now bilingual just like him!

The NYC Convergence

Chapter Thirteen

After some months passed BaoBao enjoyed herself in Washington D.C. She made many new friends in the diplomat's group and at Montrose Park. Chef Wu gave recipes to Lin and her mother so they could cook all of BaoBao's favorite dishes.

One could say that BaoBao was now assimilated. She 'fit' into American culture. BaoBao understood English commands: She would come when called. She would close the door behind her. She would bark, "Hello" in English. She ran to the door when Lin said, "BaoBao do you want to go for a walk?"

When children at the park remarked how 'good looking' she was, she understood and slowly batted her eyelashes at them and nudged closer so they could pet her. She became a notorious flirt and everyone was delighted when they saw her. Good food, daily walks, play-dates with Bo and Sunny, and a steady stream of new doggie friends made her feel happy.

She wanted to do something to 'give back.' BaoBao wondered if she could help other immigrant dogs adjust to life in America? She wanted to help them meet new friends to share their stories with. So, BaoBao organized a party in New York City.

The *United Nations Headquarters*, *Ellis Island*, *Central Park*, and *Broadway* were all there. The great get-together would take place in September when the tourist season slowed down.

She wondered how to inform the international dogs about the event. BaoBao decided to start a blog with Lin's help. Her paws were too big to strike the keys so she dictated the messages and Lin typed.

Lihua's diplomatic status also proved helpful. The *State Department, Office of Immigration,* provided a list of foreign pets who immigrated to the US. These dogs represented a convergence of cultures, personalities, breeds, and talents!

Señor Don Diego received his invitation via the blog and always ready to party, replied, "YES!"

A ticker-tape parade was planned. On the big day, all the dogs wore vests or sweaters in their national colors. Family members carried international flags. A large crowd watched the parade because New Yorkers adore doggies.

Nomsa sat on a shiny red NYC fire engine for the route down 5th Avenue to Central Park. She was well-known for cheering up firefighters and raising their spirits. The Cape Town Firefighters surprised her at the park and cheered her on.

After the parade a picnic was planned featuring international cuisine prepared by top chefs. The United Nations Headquarters and Ellis Island were toured. Comedians from

'*Saturday Night Live*' volunteered to be doggie walkers. After a walk in the theatre district, all the dogs gathered at NYC's *Hilton* for pets. Rolf was informed about the NYC gathering from Kurt and Karl. The group needed security so he was in!

When Rolf arrived at the hotel he met with security guards and checked the closed circuit TV cameras. His eyes were fixed on the revolving doors. He observed everyone who entered. There were dozens of NYC policemen and policewomen walking their beats and Rolf loved seeing them.

For dinner the group feasted on all natural *Blue Buffalo Salmon* dog food and all natural chicken jerky. Afterwards, BaoBao led a discussion on the challenges pets face when moving to a foreign country and how to overcome them.

Everyone appreciated the advice and BaoBao was made their official representative to Congress. That was possible because she was now a naturalized citizen.

Bolero danced the tango with Sofia and Romero. Hue shared stories about the generations of Hue's from Vietnam. Billy showed videos of himself surfing the big waves and saving lives. Cleo's American-born puppies demonstrated their bilingual barking skills and bi-cultural knowledge. They were intelligent doggies and she was proud of them.

    Malcolm and Murdoch found their way around the hotel within fifteen minutes. The M's told tales about running wild through Richmond, hiding under tables in the pub and their fabulous trip to St. Thomas.

    Mimi accepted the invitation only if Bud her best friend could come, too. Aashka helped all the dogs relax through yoga and meditation. She taught them to hum, "*Om.*"

    Finally, Viktor arrived from Minneapolis! He had just finished writing a mystery about a clever double-agent from St. Petersburg who was exposed as a spy, by his dog. The dog was given asylum in the U.S. and put into the witness protection program.

Viktor never forgot Russia or Natasha or Yakov who still lived there. Every New Year's Eve he sipped vodka from a shot glass and toasted his family and friends, old and new, "*Заңружбу*" to friendship!

The End

Passports for Pets

Author's Notes

The genre of this book is informational fiction.

All of the names of people and dogs were created from lists of common and/or popular names from countries of origin. The characters are fictional and not based on any known persons or pets.

This story about dogs and their exploits is purely fictional. However, since dogs have different personalities and skills some traits may apply. For example there are police dogs, dancing tango dogs, actor dogs and surfer dogs.

All the words, terms, references, and places in italics are true and can be searched on the internet for more information. For example go to YouTube to see a video of the Royal Military Tatoo, surfing events, firefighters, or dancing dogs.

About the Author:

Linda Marie MacLeod is a communications expert living in St. Cloud, Minnesota. Besides writing, she enjoys facilitating English for visiting Asian scholars and supporting women and girls' issues through the American Association of University Women.

Ms. MacLeod has earned a MS, Mass Communications, St. Cloud State University, and a BA, Speech-Communication & French, the University of Minnesota.

Made in the USA
Columbia, SC
07 May 2017